The MONKEY PIRATES

Coming soon . . .

IT'S THEM MONKEY PIRATES AGAIN!

The MONKEY PIRATES

by Mark Skelton

Illustrated by Ben Redlich

EGMONT

EGMONT

We bring stories to life

The Monkey Pirates first published 2009
by Egmont UK Limited,
239 Kensington High Street London W8 6SA

Text copyright © 2009 Mark Skelton
Illustrations copyright © 2009 Ben Redlich

The moral rights of the author and illustrator have been asserted

ISBN 978 1 4052 4393 3

1 3 5 7 9 10 8 6 4 2

www.egmont.co.uk

A CIP catalogue record for this title is available
from the British Library

Printed and bound in Great Britain by the CPI Group

WARNING!
Contains some Monkey Pirate swearing and scenes of a Monkey Pirate nature!

CONTENTS

A SHANTY TO START

What shall we do with dem Monkey Pirates?

What shall we do with dem Monkey Pirates?

What shall we do with dem Monkey Pirates?

Travelling in a wardrobe!

Way-hay, up they rises,

Way-hay, up they rises,

Way-hay, up they rises,

With bananas in their bellies!

THE VERY FIRST BIT

'Bananas and barnacles!' are the two words that start this book. This is slightly surprising when you consider all the other words that exist out there (such as 'crocodile', 'spoon', 'boo!' and 'hello'). You may ask, 'Who would say something like "bananas and barnacles"?' which is a thumpingly good question, and the

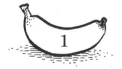

answer is actually a thumpingly brilliant one. Monkey Pirates would!

But if you are scared by adventure, frightened by hairiness and don't like Monkey Pirate swearing, then STOP RIGHT HERE!! This book is for people who are hairy-hugging, adventurous, danger-loving and crazy! And so, to all you brave boys and girls still reading, let's get going!

Linoleum-on-the-Naze was a sleepy village that rarely bothered to wake up, even after the alarm clock had gone off and all the birds

had set off to work. It was also the village where Emily Jane lived.

Emily Jane was a very unusual girl. A girl with a very lively imagination. A girl who loved adventures. A girl who would love meeting a bunch of Monkey Pirates, in fact. She was also a girl who was long on loveliness but short on height. She was sunny like the sunniest day ever, and she was never cloudy or even a bit rainy in the afternoons.

Her smile was shiny and her hair blonde, and she had eyes of blue and cheeks of pink

(what a colourful girl she was).

Emily Jane also knew a thing or two, such

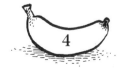

4

as how many beans made five (a bean, a half bean, a bean and a half, plus two beans), as well as who had invented time travel.

However, there were a few things that she didn't know, including why don't sheep shrink in the rain? Why is the alphabet in that order? And what on earth had happened to her Uncle Bartholomew?

Uncle Bartholomew was Emily Jane's most favourite uncle. He had a great big grey beard the size of a small English village, with enough room in it to hide animals. And as he never

brushed it there was a real possibility that it contained a few badgers, or at least a squirrel or two. Plus he was an inventor.

Uncle Bartholomew had invented many things. He was the inventor of the shoe (although this is being questioned by cobblers worldwide) and vinegar-flavoured toothpaste. He also claimed to have invented the banana, the wardrobe and time travel.

But then Uncle Bartholomew had suddenly disappeared. And all Emily Jane knew was that he had vanished while he was in the middle of

varnishing his wardrobe.

Emily Jane had not only inherited her uncle's huge imagination and sense of adventure, but also his half-varnished wardrobe. It stood in her bedroom and it always reminded her that some relatives are very easily misplaced.

Emily Jane missed her Uncle Bartholomew more than anything. She missed his humphilated laugh, his beard and his inventions. She was determined to find every bit of him.

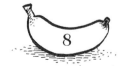

One other thing Emily Jane knew nothing of was the existence of the Monkey Pirates.

THE NEXT BIT

Our story begins one evening in September. (Actually, the story started on the first page with the bit that went 'Bananas and barnacles!' but anyway.) It was a very windy September evening. So windy that it would surprise your brain and make it very draughty for your thoughts and ideas. It was on this windy

evening when a happening happened to happen to Emily Jane.

It was getting late and Emily Jane was lying in bed trying to get to sleep. Sometimes sleep is a strange thing and will not visit you when you are hoping it will, but rather it watches from above your head, just to be slightly irritating.

Anyway, there was Emily Jane lying there and there was sleep watching her, when suddenly there was a scratching noise.

It started like the sort of noise you might

expect from a small rodent, say, a mouse, from
inside a cardboard box, say, a cornflake box.

The noise got slightly louder and then changed to a rattle. If you can imagine a rattling noise like a baby's rattle then this would not be very useful, as it sounded more like the rattle of a window frame in a very strong wind.

The rattle turned into a whooping noise. 'And all this,' thought Emily Jane, 'coming from my wardrobe.'

Emily Jane tried to ignore the noise but it was impossible. Very impossible.

'I should investigate,' Emily Jane said to herself after a few moments. She swung her legs out of

bed and slipped her feet into her slippers. She then got her dressing gown and dressed in it.

Creeping across the room, she wondered what she might find. Images of monsters, dragons, dwarves and midgets came into her mind. She did, after all, have a very lively imagination.

She crept as quietly as she could towards the mysterious noises – more silently than a panther in fluffy cotton socks.

Emily Jane reached the wardrobe doors and placed her hand on a handle. She paused and

counted to three. 'One . . . two . . . three.'

Suddenly the doors of the wardrobe burst open and with a crash out fell twelve monkeys of various shapes and sizes, wearing hats and eye patches and stuff.

Emily Jane was shocked. Her mouth fell open and she stared at the monkeys. She looked just as you would expect a small girl who has just seen twelve monkeys falling out of her wardrobe to look.

The monkeys looked up at Emily Jane from the floor where they had landed. They looked

much the way you would expect a group of monkeys who have just tumbled out of a wardrobe to look.

So, so far, everything looked pretty much as you would expect.

Emily Jane swallowed hard before trying to speak. 'What . . . who are you?' she asked.

'Aaaaaaarrrgh,' said the one wearing the biggest hat, 'we be the Monkey Pirates.'

The other eleven monkeys nodded. Then they started to explore Emily Jane's bedroom, sniffing at things and looking under her bed.

'Oh,' said Emily Jane. 'And what were you doing in my wardrobe?'

The first monkey, who Emily Jane decided must be the Captain of the Monkey Pirates, looked back from where they had just appeared. 'Oh, it just sometimes 'appens like that,' he said. 'Anyways, we were only borrowin' it to travel through time and space. No need to be getting funny about it. Bananas and barnacles!'

'I don't understand,' said Emily Jane.

Another monkey, a rather fat and short

18

one, spoke this time. 'Aaaarrrgh, well, we use people's wardrobes to travel around by. It be like our ship,' he explained. 'This way we can go in search of treasure. Yellow treasure. Yellow, bendy treasure.'

'And we fly the flag of the Monkey Pirates,' said the Captain. With that the Captain lifted his very large hat and pulled out a flag that had a monkey's head on it over a pair of crossed bananas. He waved it in the air while the other monkeys did a jig and sang a song. The song that they sang went like this:

Hey ho, we're the Banana Buccaneers,

We're the monkeys that you fears,

Out of wardrobes we appears,

Searching for yellow souvenirs.

When they had come to an end the crew all shouted together, 'Bananas and barnacles!'

Emily Jane grinned at them. The Monkey Pirates had obviously finished with the song and went back to scratching, sniffing and

peering around Emily Jane's room.

'What a great song!' commented Emily Jane.

'Anyways,' said the Captain, 'we are on a journey.'

Emily Jane was intrigued. 'Where are you going?' she asked.

One of the Monkey Pirates winked with his one good eye and said, 'We're off to find bananas!'

Another one said, 'Neep splay clump flet tremple.'

Emily Jane was confused.

One of the other crew members nodded at these words and said, 'Aaaaarrrgh, reckons you be right there, Gobbledygook' and mimed peeling a banana and eating it. He rubbed his fat and hairy belly and licked his lips.

'And all thanks to the King of the Monkey Pirates,' added the Captain.

'Who?' asked Emily Jane.

'Aaaaarrrrgh! He be a magnificent man and a man of great intelligence and of a great beard,' explained the Captain. 'He be an inventor. He knows many things.'

'Would he know where my Uncle Bartholomew is, do you think?' asked Emily Jane.

'I reckon he might,' said the Captain.

Emily Jane thought travelling in a wardrobe full of monkeys would be very strange, but fun. What if the King of the Monkey Pirates could really help her find her Uncle Bartholomew? What if he knew where he had gone and if he had truly varnished himself and then vanished? And what if sausages could be used to find your way at night?

23

She was certain that she should meet their king. While her imagination carried on being imaginative by itself she found herself saying, 'Can I come as well to meet the king?'

At this point there was murmuring within the ranks and one Monkey Pirate looked gravely at the Captain and said, 'But, Cap'in, having a lass on a journey would be bad luck. Our trip would be cursed. Nar, nay, never says me.'

'Aaaarrrrgh! But you think everything is bad luck, Piffle, you scurvy dog,' replied the

Captain. "Sides, I likes the cut of her jib.'

'Aaaarrrrgh!' said another. 'Shut yer noise.'
He flicked the first monkey around the back
of the head. This made all the others laugh.

The Captain laughed a huge laugh but
then suddenly became very serious. 'You'll be
needing to pay your passage, lass.'

Emily Jane was no ordinary girl and she was
now clever enough to know what all Monkey
Pirates want. She disappeared from the room,
crept downstairs and returned with a bunch
of bananas.

'Now that will be doing nicely,' said the Captain as he took them from her.

The rest of the Monkey Pirates had already begun amusing themselves as Monkey Pirates tend to do, scratching, burping, swinging from the light shade and bouncing on the bed. ('And I'm always told off for bouncing on the bed,' thought Emily Jane longingly.)

'And do you all have names?' she asked the Captain.

'Aaaaarrgh! We do indeed, missy,' said the Captain, whom Emily Jane thought

looked particularly important in his hat. Her imagination suggested that he looked like a giraffe that had just discovered the meaning of life. (If you're not sure what that would look like, ask your mum or dad.)

'My name,' said the Captain, 'is Captain Banana S. Piranha* on accounts that I gobbles so many bananas. And these are my Banana Buccaneers,' he said, pointing to the rest of the crew. (*The 'S' stood for Something.)

The Monkey Pirates stopped what they were doing and looked in Emily Jane's direction.

Then they all lined up and went,

'Aaaaarrrrgh!' in the very best

pirate way and

then called

out their

names as

if from

a great

big Pirate

School

register.

CAPTAIN BANANA
S. PIRANHA

28

'Aarrgh! Piffle,' said the first one.

'Aaarrrgh! Tripe,' said the second.

'Aaaarrrrgh! Balderdash,' said the next.

    'Aaaaarrrrrgh! Tosh,' said the
one after the next one.

       'Aaaaaarrrrrrgh!

PIFFLE   TRIPE   BALDERDASH

Gobbledygook,' said another.

'Aaaaaaarrrrrrrgh! Gibberish,' said the one next to the another one.

'Aaaaaaarrrrrrrrgh! Drivel,' said one of the last ones.

'Aaaaaaaaaarrrrrrrrrgh! Twaddle,' said the

one standing next to him.

'Aaaaaaaaaarrrrrrrrrrgh! Guff,' said the one next to the one standing next to him.

'Aaaaaaaaaarrrrrrrrrrrgh! Poppycock,' said the second to last.

DRIVEL

TWADDLE   GUFF   POPPYCOCK   DAVE

There was a slight pause.

'Ummmm, Dave,' said the last one.

Dave was very new to the job.

Emily Jane giggled. 'I'm very pleased to meet you all. My name is Emily Jane,' she said.

Emily Jane considered the Monkey Pirates. She considered the frilliness of the frills on their shirts and the stripy-ness of the stripes on their trousers. She considered the hat-ness of their hats and the general pirate-ness of them all. Overall, she was pretty impressed.

'A fine crew and makes no mistake,' said the Captain, and then added, 'shame about Poppycock.' He leant towards Emily. 'Not been the luckiest of Monkey Pirates,' he whispered.

Emily Jane had to agree that Poppycock didn't look like he had had a lot of luck. He had one wooden leg and a hook instead of a hand and a patch over one eye. And he had wooden teeth and a false tin ear. In truth, there was not a great deal left of Poppycock, but what was left was all true Monkey Pirate.

'And Piffle,' continued the Captain, 'doesn't tend to look on the positive side a great deal.'

'Bad luck comes from too much of that sort of looking,' said Piffle. 'Only one way to get rid of bad luck.' He suddenly turned round three times on the spot and tweaked his nose. 'This journey is going to be cursed, you mark me words!' he said and span round three times, tweaking his nose again.

Emily Jane thought this was rather funny and giggled.

'Of course, I do 'ave a parrot as well,' said

the Captain. 'A fine bird, make no mistake. Deaf as a post, mind, after working in a circus and being fired out of a cannon every night.'

The Captain suddenly yelled out, '**MONTGOMERY!**', making Emily Jane jump.

Almost immediately, nothing happened.

'**MONTGOMERY!!!**' the Captain yelled again, this time a bit louder.

Emily Jane was sure that her parents would hear all this commotion and she poked her head out of the door to check everything was all right. Luckily, the television was very

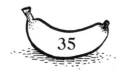

loud and they hadn't been disturbed. When she turned back into her room she saw that after all that noise there was a distinct lack of parrot.

'See, I told ye he was deaf!' said the Captain. 'Anyways,' he continued, 'we can't stand around here all night. Let's get going. All aboard, my banana buccaneering beauties!'

'Bananas and barnacles!' shouted the rest.

'Yes,' said Emily Jane getting very excited, 'bananas and barnacles!'

They were off!!!

A BIT WITH A LOT OF NEW WORDS IN IT AND WITH SOME OF THE OLD ONES, BUT IN A DIFFERENT ORDER

'Travelling in a wardrobe with twelve monkeys dressed as pirates is going to be very odd,' thought Emily Jane. And of course she was absolutely right.

There is something else that you should know

about travelling in a wardrobe and that is:

A) It's very dark.

And when you travel in a wardrobe with monkeys in it, it is also:

B) A bit hairy.

And when you are travelling in a wardrobe with Monkey Pirates in it, it is also:

C) Full of pirate talk.

Inside the wardrobe the Monkey Pirates called out instructions:

'Splice the main brace!' said the Captain, although he wasn't too sure what a main brace was or how to splice one.

'Weigh the anchor!' said Guff, which was something he had heard that pirates say a lot.

'Shiver me timbers,' said Poppycock, who wasn't exactly sure how to make anybody's timbers shiver.

'Mumpull flam trump!' suggested Gobbledygook.

'Aaaarrrrgh!' agreed Gibberish.

'Umm, comb your hair?' suggested Dave,

which Emily Jane thought was a bit strange, coming from a pirate.

'I still says that this be bad luck,' said Piffle.

'Shut up!' said the rest.

'That's total mug whack!' swore Twaddle.

There was a fizzing and a buzzing noise and Emily Jane could feel the wardrobe move. It wobbled and then there was a sudden surge. Her stomach felt that it was going to be left behind in the rush but it managed to keep up with the rest of her. They were definitely off!

Emily Jane was squished from all sides by Monkey Pirates. There was a coughing and a sneezing coming from one of them. Emily Jane turned to see that the last cough had made his trousers fall down. He quickly pulled them up. 'Sorry about that, lass. I've not been too well of late,' he said, coughing and spluttering.

Now, Monkey Pirate trousers come in two sizes – Monkey Pirate standard and Monkey Pirate extra large. This Monkey Pirate, Tripe, was neither of these and he struggled to keep

his trousers up, in spite of his pirate belt and a pair of pirate braces.

'Oh dear, I'm sorry to hear that,' Emily Jane said sympathetically.

'Ignore Tripe,' suggested the Captain. 'He's always ill.'

'Grumple flet trumple stran!' said Gobbledy-gook, looking at Emily Jane.

Emily Jane didn't know what to say.

'Aaaarghh! Mostly I reckon you're right there,' said Gibberish, nodding at him and then whistling. He waved a bugle around and

Emily Jane thought he might play a tune, but he didn't. It was a bugle that he never played, but he kept it with him at all times, as it was a present from a one-eyed dog called Lazarus Bones. You don't often get presents from one-eyed dogs, so they were always worth keeping hold of when you did.

'Don't worry about them,' said the Captain. 'Only Gibberish can understand Gobbledygook.'

'Oh. Well, hello, both of you,' said Emily Jane.

Then there was a slight rumbling noise close to her ear. It came from another of the Monkey Pirates.

'That's Guff,' the Captain said.

Emily Jane smiled at Guff, who just burped. Guff was always full of beans (or, rather, bananas) and could burp tunes, a skill that

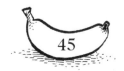

was much admired by the other Monkey Pirates, as you can probably well imagine.

After Guff's contribution Emily Jane was pleased when their journey came to an end. With much shaking, rattling, rolling, monkey noises and obviously a few cries of 'Bananas and barnacles!' they came to rest.

The doors sprang open and out fell twelve monkeys and one little girl.

They found themselves in a very large and empty bedroom, but none of them knew where they were.

THE QUEEN'S BIT

While Emily Jane and the Monkey Pirates were unsure of their whereabouts, the Queen of England was very aware of her whereabouts. She was at home in her palace.

The Queen's palace was not only very big and royal, it also had a lot of rooms, many of which had wardrobes in them.

It was one of these wardrobes which had just sprung open and spilt a cocktail of little girl and monkey (one part girl to twelve parts monkey) on to the floor.

The Queen was far too busy doing Queen-like things, with a nice cup of tea, in a faraway room in the palace to hear their arrival.

However, a palace guard walking along one of the corridors thought he heard something, and stopped.

'Now that,' he thought to himself, 'sounded like a large quantity of monkeys falling out of

a Royal wardrobe.' As this did not seem very likely, he chuckled to himself and carried on, ignoring the entire thing.

Back in the large, empty room, the Monkey Pirates were very excited, while Emily Jane was very confused.

'Where on earth are we? I thought we were going to meet the King of the Monkey Pirates?' she asked out loud, although nobody paid her any attention.

Emily Jane scrambled to her feet and went over to a big bay window with a large balcony.

Carefully, she peered out.

A group of guardsmen

wearing big furry hats and

sitting on horses was not what

Emily Jane had been expecting

to see. But that was exactly

what she did see.

'We're in the Queen's palace!' she exclaimed in a loud voice. She also noticed that they had set off during the evening but had arrived during the day. 'Those monkeys must have done some time travel as well,' she said to herself, impressed.

'Bananas and barnacles! The Queen's palace! Lots of treasure then, me

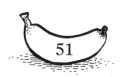

beauties!' announced the Captain, and the other monkeys cheered, whooped and chattered.

'Oh no! You mustn't!' said Emily Jane. 'You can't take things off the Queen of England!'

But before the words 'the Queen of England' had left Emily Jane's mouth, most of the monkeys had opened the door and had run out of sight.

'Oh no!' thought Emily Jane, and as this seemed such a very good thought to have, she said it out loud as well.

52

'Oh no!!'

The only Monkey Pirate left in the room nodded in agreement. Emily Jane looked at him.

'I'm Dave,' he said, sticking out his hand.

Dave was different from the other Monkey Pirates. He stood quietly in his neatly ironed shirt and trousers and his recently combed hair, which was nicely parted in the middle.

'Hello, Dave,' Emily Jane said, shaking his hand.

'The others do that sort of thing quite a

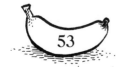

lot,' Dave said, sighing.

'Do they?' asked Emily Jane.

'Yes. They're quite, umm, excitable,' Dave explained.

'Yes, I noticed that,' agreed Emily Jane.

'And they do like their bananas,' he continued.

'You seem very different from the rest,' Emily Jane remarked, looking at his shirt, waistcoat and small hat.

'Er, yes,' said Dave.

'How on earth did you ever become a Monkey Pirate?' asked Emily Jane.

'Well,' said Dave, 'I asked if they were a travelling theatre group and they all went "Aaarrgh!" I took that as being a yes.'

'Oh, I see,' said Emily Jane.

'As I thought that they were going to put on some interesting plays, I asked if I could join them,' he continued.

'Did they all go "Aaarrgh"?' asked Emily Jane.

Dave nodded. 'So I followed them. I've been with them ever since.' He then gave a small sigh. 'I've been *trying* to be a Monkey Pirate, but I don't know if I'm cut out for it. Sometimes I just want to be in the woods, playing a banjo with the squirrels and rabbits, or in bed with a good book.

'To be honest,' he continued, 'I wish I was better at jigs and burping and things. But I must admit I much prefer tea and biscuits to bananas.'

'Well, I'm sure you'll soon learn,' said Emily Jane. 'It's quite difficult to burp exactly when you want to.'

Cheering up a little, Dave said, 'Would you like to see my stamp collection?' He pulled a stamp album from his pocket.

'Oh, that would be lovely,' said Emily Jane. 'But shall we look a little later? I think I need

57

to see what the rest of the crew are doing.'

She smiled at Dave and left the room to look for the other Monkey Pirates.

Dave was already admiring a small red stamp that was one of his favourites.

A BIT ABOUT BANANAS

Here is a bit of a break for all you readers who probably are feeling a little peckish now. Right, who fancies a nice cup of tea and a biscuit? Oh look, you've got some of those nice chocolate ones.

As we're just sitting here, you might as well consider what Monkey Pirates like to eat. Here is a typical menu for them:

BREAKFAST

A banana, a banana and banana jam on a toasted banana.

LUNCH

A banana, a banana, a banana, a banana, a banana and a nice cup of tea.

DINNER

A banana, a banana, a banana, a
banana, a banana, a banana and
a banana, all served with a banana
pie with banana gravy.

I think this gives you the general idea.

Anyway, back to the action.

ANOTHER BIT

By now, the Queen had finished her cup of tea, but she was still doing Queen-like things. She called for her footman, who came immediately and stood next to her with both his foots (sorry, feet).

'I think that I would very much like,' the Queen announced regally and royally, 'a nice

banana split.'

'Yes, Your Majesty,' said the footman, bowing, and he left the room in a flurry of frock coat.

Now, it takes a lot to surprise a Royal footman. For instance, a crocodile in a wig holding a balloon and leaning against

a piano would probably do it. Or, indeed, a monkey with a patch over its eye, in a big hat and long boots, running along the banisters of the Royal staircase, followed by a small girl in a dressing gown would probably do it too.

While the footman had never come across a crocodile in the Royal palace, he could have sworn that he had just seen a monkey and a girl. He shook his head and rubbed his eyes.

'No, no, that's not right,' he said to himself. 'I'm working too hard,' he thought. 'I must be tired.'

He used the same excuse when he saw a second monkey, in similar dress, leaving the Royal kitchens with a bunch of bananas over its shoulder.

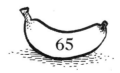

Meanwhile, Emily Jane was worried about what the Monkey Pirates were up to. She started to try to round them up before they did too much damage.

However, all of Emily Jane's chasing was of little use. If you are ever asked to catch a bunch of monkeys dressed as pirates, just say, 'No, thank you.' Monkey Pirates are more difficult to grasp than fractions and even more slippery than banana skins. They had scattered throughout the palace in search of their yellow, bendy treasure.

Emily Jane eventually sat down, exhausted, on the floor outside one of the Royal rooms.

There was a Monkey Pirate hanging upside down from the ceiling on a Royal chandelier near her. He was wearing a hat and from his belt hung a whacking stick. (Monkey Pirates do not carry swords but have whacking sticks instead. They use them for whacking all things annoying, horrible or just generally irksome.)

She turned her head to one side to try and see the monkey's face the right way up.

'Now you're Poppycock, aren't you?' ventured Emily Jane.

'Piffle!!' he replied, offended by this suggestion. 'I'm Balderdash.'

Emily Jane apologised for her mistake.

You would probably have a lot of questions for a Monkey Pirate like Balderdash. However, a word of advice: don't ask any questions about fruit flies. Balderdash hates fruit flies. He hates their long licky tongues and their buzzy noises. He particularly hates the way they make bananas go all soft and yucky. He

will always say 'Dem bibbly shuck things Cabbage-bum creatures. I 'ates dem' whenever they are mentioned.

You might have other questions about the Monkey Pirates and you might well ask,

'Have you always been Monkey Pirates?' to which the answer would be, 'Yes, once we escaped from the circus.'

Emily Jane asked Balderdash that question and his reply was, 'Aaaarrgh, I dunno!'

Balderdash had been a Monkey Pirate for as long as he could remember, but the problem was that he had a very bad memory. He couldn't even remember much about what he did yesterday.

Another question might be, 'Have you always been together?' to which, of course, the reply would be, 'Yes, we were together as part of a circus. A Mister Phileas Claxton owned the circus and the Monkey Pirates

were one of the main acts, along with a parrot called Montgomery, who was fired out of a small cannon every night. The huge explosions played havoc with his hearing, though.'

However, Balderdash's reply was, 'Aaaaarrrgh, now, can't really remember that bit.'

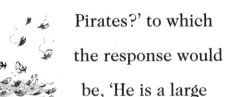

And a further question might be, 'Who is the King of the Monkey Pirates?' to which the response would be, 'He is a large

friendly man with a beard who saved us from the circus, much to the huge annoyance of Mister Phileas Claxton. It was then that the Monkey Pirates made him their King.'

Balderdash's response was, 'Aaaarrgh, he be a man . . . I think.'

So, at this point you know a lot more and Emily Jane has a lot more to learn.

However, Emily Jane was a very conscientious young girl, so she took out a small notebook and pencil from her dressing-gown pocket and wrote a few notes. 'That's

something that might go towards making a Fairly Useful Guide to the Monkey Pirates,' she thought.

Balderdash did, however, have something to show Emily Jane. He smiled a very special smile and Emily Jane noticed his teeth for the first time. His mouth looked a bit like a piano, with one white tooth followed by a black one followed by a white one and so on and so forth. She made no attempt to play a tune on them though. Luckily, she also made no attempt to mention fruit flies, so Balderdash didn't say,

'Dem bibbly shuck things. Cabbage-bum creatures. I 'ates dem.' What he *did* say, in a rather mysterious manner, was, 'Since you have joined us, you must have a treasure that you are seeking.'

Then he handed Emily Jane a small telescope. 'Take a look through this here telescope. It's a thing of ingenious cleverness. It was invented for us by the King of the Monkey Pirates,' he continued.

Emily Jane put it to her eye and was amazed to see a strange vision at the end of the

 telescope. Instead of close-ups of the inside of the Queen's palace she could only see a man.

She looked closer and saw he was a man with a very large grey beard with a little bit of varnish on it. It was Uncle Bartholomew!

'Do you know this man?' she asked.

'Don't know – everyone sees different things. They sees things from their past or

future. It be a time-telescope,' Balderdash explained.

'Well, I can see a man with a big but slightly varnished grey beard,' said Emily Jane excitedly. Perhaps she was getting closer to finding her Uncle Bartholomew!

'Aaaaarrrgh, I reckon he sounds familiar,' said Balderdash.

'So am I looking at the past or the future? How does it work?' Emily Jane continued.

Balderdash just shrugged and said, 'Aaarrgh, dunno!'

So, as you can see, Balderdash didn't really know a great deal.

Emily Jane went to return the telescope to Balderdash but he just said, 'It be yours now.'

Emily Jane thanked him and placed it in her dressing-gown pocket.

Just then there was a loud Royal voice from behind one of the Royal doors.

'What do you mean, no bananas?!' shouted the Queen.

Queens (and Kings as well, for that matter)

78

were used to certain things, such as crowns, robes and ceremonies but they were not used to not getting their puddings when they asked for them.

'Quick!' said Emily Jane. 'We need to get going.'

A BIT NEARER TO THE END

By now, the Monkey Pirates were all over the place and all over the palace and Emily Jane was trying her very best to control things. These Monkey Pirates certainly made her laugh but this wasn't helping her find her uncle.

She reached the top of the stairs and saw a

lot of Monkey Pirates running around, swinging off things and generally up to no good whatsoever.

The Captain was sitting on top of a grandfather clock in the hallway making very rude raspberry noises at all the Royal servants that passed below him. None of them said anything, or mentioned anything to anyone else, just like the footman hadn't mentioned the monkeys he'd seen to anyone else. They all thought that perhaps they were going mad and it was best not to discuss such things.

This goes to show how a group of Monkey Pirates can come and go as they please, even in the Queen's palace.

'You must come down at once,' said Emily Jane to the Captain. 'This is very naughty.'

'Yer think so?' said the Captain. 'Bananas and barnacles!' he exclaimed.

'Yes,' said Emily Jane. 'Some of your crew are outside, sitting on top of the guardsmen's hats. Let's get them back in the wardrobe. I should really be getting home. Perhaps we can look for my Uncle Bartholomew another time.'

The Captain eventually jumped down from the grandfather clock. 'Aaaaarrgh, let me see,' he said.

He took out something small which he examined very closely.

'What's that?' asked Emily Jane.

'It be a banana compass,' he explained. He showed it to Emily Jane. It was a small mechanical gadget with a tiny arrow that spun round and round over a very interesting dial. The dial had pictures of bananas on it at regular intervals around the face (the face was

that of a grinning monkey).

'It points to all bananas north, south, east and west,' the Captain explained. 'Looks like we've got 'em all now! Let's go!'

Emily Jane was relieved to hear this and she began to think again about her uncle. 'I would very much like to meet the King of the Monkey Pirates,' she said as she handed back the compass.

'Would you now?' said the Captain.

'Yes,' said Emily Jane. 'I think he could help me in my search for my Uncle Bartholomew.'

'Aaaarrgh, we all have a treasure we're searching for. Anyway, it's time for us to go,' the Captain said, changing the subject.

He and Emily Jane began rounding up the rest of his crew.

The Captain leant out of a window and shouted out to the Monkey Pirates sitting on the guardsmen's hats. 'Time to be going!'

'Aaaarrgh, it be bad luck to outstay yer welcome,' agreed Piffle.

'That be complete fuggle-bung!' swore Twaddle.

Gobbledygook asked 'Klimp joop?' but nobody knew what he was on about and so they ignored him.

Guff just burped.

They all joined Emily Jane and the Captain and went searching for the others.

They found Tripe in the kitchen. He sneezed and then pulled up his trousers and joined the rest of them.

Tosh also appeared in the kitchen. Tosh was by far the dirtiest of all the Monkey Pirates, which was quite an achievement. He

always brought with him two fleas (both called
Pete) who had made a home on him.

'Looks like we're off again, Pete,' said Pete.

'Yes, looks like it, Pete,' agreed Pete.

Tosh and the two Petes left the kitchen and

joined the others.

Poppycock hopped along on his wooden leg and caught up with the growing numbers of Monkey Pirates.

Dave had been waiting patiently. He was still sitting next to the wardrobe when the others reappeared.

By the time the Queen visited the Royal kitchens to get an explanation for the lack of bananas, Emily Jane had managed to get all of the Monkey Pirates back into the Royal wardrobe.

'We need to go,' said Emily Jane. 'You've got all the bananas here,' she explained.

'Aaaaarrgh! Let's be off in search of more treasures, me hearties,' suggested the Captain.

All the Monkey Pirates agreed with a loud **'Bananas and barnacles!'** and they were off, leaving behind a very bemused Royal household and one seriously unamused Queen.

8

A BIT OF A SHORT CUT

It was very cramped on the way back and at one point there was a strange noise, a bit like a small trumpet, and Emily Jane noticed a strong smell of bananas. 'Probably Guff again,' she thought.

The return trip was cheered up when the monkeys sang the second verse of their sea shanty:

Hey ho, we're the Banana Buccaneers,

Travelling from there to here,

We makes bananas disappear,

And dem fruit flies are just mutineers!

As the song ended, Balderdash muttered, 'Dem bibbly shuck things. Cabbage-bum creatures. I 'ates dem.'

When the wardrobe doors opened Emily Jane was expecting her own bedroom, or a clue in her search for her uncle, so she was a little surprised by what followed. The doors

opened and yet again they all tumbled out on to the floor. But instead of her bedroom, they had arrived in a strange room that was dark, dusty and smelt rather peculiarly (like a mixture of shoes, vinegar and bananas).

'Where are we now?' Emily Jane asked.

Now, although the Monkey Pirates were very bad at navigation, they did all know where they were this time.

'We're back at the Professor's. He be a great man,' explained the Captain.

'Why is that?' asked Emily Jane.

'It be bad luck to speak too much about the Professor,' said Piffle before anyone could speak.

Poppycock rolled his one good eye and shook his head, making his wooden teeth shake and his tin ear rattle.

The Monkey Pirates all began leaping about in an excited way, apart from Drivel, who turned to Emily Jane. However, because he had bad eyesight he started to explain things to a hat stand instead.

Emily Jane tapped him on the shoulder and

coughed politely.

'Aaaarrgh, and you can wait,' he said over his shoulder. 'Can't yer sees I be talking to the lass now?'

Emily Jane didn't want to point out Drivel's mistake so she simply eavesdropped on his conversation with the hat stand.

'Aaaarrgh, the Professor is indeed a great man,' said Drivel (to a rather uninterested hat stand). 'He always has a welcome for us and likes to lay on great feasts.'

'How interesting,' thought Emily Jane.

'Why is he telling me all this?' thought the hat stand.

Drivel was very short-sighted. Drivel was so short-sighted that even if the letters in this book were very, very, very

BIG

he still wouldn't be able to read it. (Also because he hadn't learned to read.)

Emily Jane looked round the room. There were no electric lights. No computers. No

toasters. She guessed that they had travelled back in time and they were in a past century. One that had passed a long time ago, it must be said.

Emily Jane felt excited. 'It isn't every day that you go back in time, after all,' she thought.

The Professor lived when time itself was quite new and a little unstable on its feet; it was before electricity had been invented and so people were forced to watch television by candlelight. It was a time of steam and tall

hats and hair on men's faces. Indeed, it was a time when men with large moustaches wore tall, steam-driven hats. Probably.

However, the Monkey Pirates did assure Emily Jane of two things, which were these:

1) That coming back via another century was a short cut to her bedroom. And that
2) They meant to do it. (Although Emily Jane doubted this. She was beginning to realise that the Monkey Pirates never really knew where they would finally end

up on their journeys. That made it all the more exciting!)

The Monkey Pirates were busy laughing, shouting and aaaaarrrgh-ing, pleased at the prospect of seeing the Professor.

Emily Jane noticed row upon row of wardrobes against the opposite wall. Not only were there lots of wardrobes, there was also a parrot perched on one of the wardrobe handles. The parrot was ignoring all the commotion in the room.

The Captain looked over at the parrot. 'Aaaaarrgh, it be Montgomery,' he said.

The parrot immediately said and did nothing. Emily Jane remembered that this was the Captain's deaf parrot.

'Why are there so many wardrobes here?' asked Emily Jane.

'Because the Professor is not only a collector of wardrobes, he is also the inventor of wardrobes,' said the Captain.

Emily Jane was going to point out that the inventor of wardrobes was in fact her Uncle Bartholomew but there wasn't time.

At that very moment, one of the other wardrobe doors opened and out stepped a big man with a small grey beard (about the size of a small mammal, let's say a badger) and a big smile. He was a hulumphing great man of enormous jolliness.

Emily Jane thought there was something rather familiar about him. 'Perhaps if that beard was a lot bigger . . .' she said to herself.

The man greeted each monkey with a big friendly slap on the back and a few cries of 'Bananas and barnacles!' In fact, so big and friendly were the slaps that they caused Tripe's trousers to fall down (he pulled them back up again quickly, looking slightly embarrassed). He also coughed a little and complained about feeling poorly. It was also a slap that sent Poppycock spinning round on

his wooden leg like a hairy spinning top. However, all the Monkey Pirates were very excited to see him. 'Aaargh!' they all shouted, and the Captain waved their flag over his head.

'Glump flumpt speer toot,' said Gobbledygook to the Professor, who laughed and gave him another friendly slap.

After everyone had greeted each other, the man noticed Emily Jane. 'And who are you?' he asked, peering down at her.

'My name is Emily Jane,' she said, 'and I

have been travelling with the Monkey Pirates to look for my Uncle Bartholomew.'

'Have you now? And what does your uncle look like?' he asked.

'A big jolly man with an even bigger grey beard than yours,' she said.

The Professor laughed and stroked his own beard. 'Well, there's a coincidence,' he said. 'Beards run in my family as well. Even some of the women have grown one and they wear them for very special occasions.'

With that, he turned to the Monkey Pirates

and shouted, 'Down with fruit flies and let's eat!'

Amongst the cheers Emily Jane could just about hear one of the monkeys muttering, 'Dem bibbly shuck things. Cabbage-bum creatures. I 'ates dem.'

The Professor threw open the doors to another room to reveal a huge table straining under a large pile of bananas.

'Are these Monkey Pirates always hungry?' Emily Jane asked herself.

The answer was obviously 'yes', even just

after eating all the Royal bananas. They leapt about at the sight of the feast.

'You never know where your next banana is coming from,' noted Guff and burped.

Tripe pulled up his trousers and headed straight for the table.

'Strange he ain't ever ill when there's bananas around,' noted the Captain.

Gibberish whistled at the sight of the banana-filled table and Gobbledygook licked his lips.

'Flap trut sneer,' said Gobbledygook.

'You mostly be right there,' agreed Gibberish.

Drivel managed to go the wrong side of the door and walked straight into the wall. He squinted at the wall, shouted at it for getting in his way and then walked round to the correct side of the door and made his way to the table.

Twaddle, on seeing the banana feast, swore loudly, 'Wotpuck!! Look at that!' (Twaddle does a lot of Monkey Pirate swearing so if you are easily offended try closing your eyes when you read his bits.)

Soon all the Monkey Pirates had jumped up on to high wooden chairs and started eating and throwing the skins all over the place until the whole room was covered in banana skins.

Dave sat quietly with a cup of tea and a

chocolate HobNob.

Emily Jane laughed as the Monkey Pirates had a competition to see who could throw their banana skins the furthest. Then she took out her time-telescope and looked through it.

But it didn't appear to be working, as all she saw was a close-up of the Professor sitting at the end of the table.

The Professor was laughing a very hearty laugh like a large bear that had just been told a fantastically funny joke.

'Will I ever see my uncle again?' Emily Jane wondered. It was all very confusing. He could be anywhere. She was no closer to finding him.

She put the telescope back into her pocket and looked back at the monkeys, who were

now having a burping competition.

Guff was winning with burps that were by far the loudest and longest. The experience was a bit like being blasted by a banana-scented hairdryer. In last place was Dave, who would put his hand politely over his mouth and say 'pardon' every time he burped. Dave hadn't got the hang of the game yet, although he was trying.

Normally, Emily Jane would have tried to join in (she liked burping!), but she was lost in thoughts about her uncle.

Suddenly, the Professor appeared at her side. 'Sometimes,' he said, 'you don't know that you have found your treasure even when it's right in front of you.' And he smiled a great big smile, which was as friendly as a great big bouncing dog.

'Sometimes,' he continued, 'you have to allow time to pass before you are really sure you have found what you are looking for. And sometimes you have to discover things by yourself so you fully understand everything.'

Emily Jane looked up at him and thought,

'You're odd. Very nice, but just a bit odd.'

'How do you know the Monkey Pirates?' asked Emily Jane.

'I have known them for a long time and will know them for a long time to come. In fact, in time to come, I will help them. They always visit me when they are in this century,' the Professor said mysteriously.

'But how do you know that you will help them in the future?' asked Emily Jane.

Rather than reply, the Professor ran to the other end of the table again.

'Let's play some music!' he yelled.

'Aaarrgh!' the Monkey Pirates yelled back.

So the Captain played the mouth organ, the Professor played a nose flute and they were accompanied by Balderdash on Montgomery's ear trumpet. Gibberish whistled and Guff burped in tune. Poppycock danced and spun round on his wooden leg and sung the way you would expect someone who had a tin ear to sing. Drivel went back to chat with the hat stand, and Emily Jane twirled round and round in a jig with Tripe.

Eventually, the Professor left the room and with a very loud 'Bananas and barnacles!' he opened one of the wardrobe doors and disappeared.

Then the door opened again quickly and he poked his head around it, winked at Emily Jane and disappeared once more.

With the Professor gone and the bananas eaten, the Monkey Pirates didn't know what to do next. They all stood in the room amid the pile of banana skins.

Emily Jane made a suggestion. 'Shall we go

on another journey? I still haven't found my uncle, remember?'

The Captain obviously thought that this was a good idea and simply said, 'Come, Montgomery!'

The parrot, which hadn't moved during the entire performance, did nothing at his instruction.

The Monkey Pirates all clambered into their wardrobe, followed by Emily Jane and then followed by no parrots whatsoever.

They were off once more.

9

VERY NEARLY THE LAST BIT

This time the journey ended with the doors opening and Emily Jane and the Monkey Pirates falling out on to her bedroom floor. Emily Jane was beginning to think that there must be an easier way to travel through time and space. She was getting very bruised. She felt that wardrobes were a little bit rubbish

but she didn't say anything. She didn't want
to hurt the Monkey Pirates' feelings, after all,

because they thought it
was great fun.

The monkeys
quickly got to their
feet and dashed back
inside the wardrobe
and closed the doors
behind them. Then
the Captain poked his
head out and said,

121

'We will be back for you soon, we need to find your treasure. Bananas and barnacles!'

'Bananas and barnacles!' Emily Jane replied, waving at him. She watched the wardrobe as it rattled (this time sounding more like a baby's rattle) and grew extremely noisy. Then it fell silent.

Emily Jane peeked inside but there were no monkeys left in it. Instead, it was just filled with her normal stuff.

She sighed a big sigh. The Monkey Pirates had gone and she wasn't too sure when they

were coming back. But what an adventure she'd had!

She was very tired, so she got back into bed. Sleep quickly dropped down on to her.

Emily Jane had a dream that night. Guess what she dreamed about?

If you said 'Monkey Pirates' I'm afraid you were wrong. She actually dreamed about Pig Astronauts – pigs who were astronauts and travelled to outer space in search of cosmic truffles. When she woke up, she was surprised by the general lack of monkeys and bananas

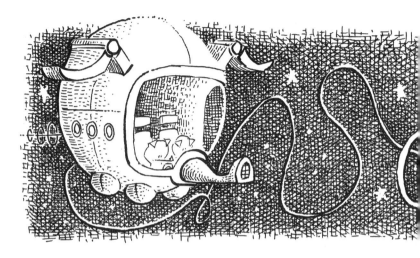

that had entered her head.

'Well,' thought Emily Jane, 'there is no accounting for dreams.' And certainly there was no accounting for her imagination.

Emily Jane sat up in bed with a slight smell of banana about her. She felt under her pillow

and found the time-telescope that Balderdash
had given her. She looked through it again
and the vision was different once more. She
could see herself with Uncle Bartholomew
and she was standing next to him. She
wondered if this was a vision of the past or the

future. It was all confusing.

But she began to feel that these odd monkeys would one day lead her to her highly bearded uncle. She could hardly wait!

She hid the telescope in one of her drawers and went downstairs. Her mum and dad were eating breakfast. For a moment Emily Jane thought about trying to explain things to them but she didn't know where to start. Instead, she decided to keep the whole thing to herself.

'Have a nice sleep?' asked her mum.

'Ummmm, yes,' replied Emily Jane, sitting down at the table.

The radio was on. 'And we are just receiving news from the Royal palace,' said the announcer. 'In an amazing development, the Queen has decided to get rid of all the Royal workers and guardsmen, because of their extremely odd behaviour.'

Mum said, 'Oh dear!'

Emily Jane looked at the radio with a great deal of surprise.

Dad grunted at something in the newspaper.

'Whatever next?' he said and tutted. 'It says here that they are selling a new toothpaste. Vinegar flavour apparently! And the sales

have gone through the roof.' He shook his head in disbelief. He then looked over the top of his newspaper and said, 'And where have all our bananas gone?'

Emily Jane just shrugged her shoulders.

THE LAST BIT

When a story comes to an end there is sometimes a moral such as 'Beware of monkeys in wardrobes' or 'Never eat anything bigger than your head'.

Sometimes there is a joke such as 'Why are Monkey Pirates scary? I don't know, they just Aaaaarrgh!'

130

Sometimes they end with a happy bit like: 'Everyone was given their own black beard to keep and the sunshine bathed all the land, wearing a rather colourful bathing cap.'

Sometimes they end with a sad bit like: 'Blackness spread across the land and huge fruit flies stalked everyday folk on their hairy legs with their buzzy noises and their long licky tongues, making everyone's bananas all soft and yucky.'

'Dem bibbly shuck things. Cabbage-bum creatures. I 'ates dem.'

But this one ends like this.

Emily Jane ate her breakfast quickly and left her mum and dad searching for the missing bananas. She got out fast to avoid any difficult questions. She then spent the rest of the day with her time-telescope and her imagination.

As time passed Emily Jane did ordinary things with her loveliness and shiny smile while her imagination did other things.

Her imagination went off to see if there would be other opportunities to meet the

Monkey Pirates and to find her beloved Uncle Bartholomew.

Her imagination knew that there would be. So from then on Emily Jane always kept her time-telescope and some bananas close to hand so she would be completely ready for the next time the Monkey Pirates fell out of her wardrobe and took her on an adventure.

Her imagination said, 'Bananas and barnacles!'

A FAIRLY USEFUL GUIDE TO THE MONKEY PIRATES (PART 1)

Your very own guide to keep, offering an essential and quick reference to a number of the Monkey Pirates. This guide should be kept handy in case you meet one or more of the Monkey Pirates.

NAME: Captain Banana S. Piranha

RANK: Captain

DISTINGUISHING FEATURES:
A huge hat of a rather resplendent nature

LIKES: Bananas, some shiny things, King of the Monkey Pirates, wardrobes and time travel

DISLIKES: Phileas Claxton

FAVOURITE ROCK STAR: Twain Zenith

SECRET FACT 1: The 'S' in his name stands for Something (apparently)

AMBITIONS: To own the world's largest banana and become a member of Royalty

SECRET FACT 2:
He believes that he is related to Royalty

136

SECRET FACT 3:

He's completely wrong about that Royalty thing

GREATEST MOMENT: Defeating the Octa-Snotty-Pus, the Flabbyfartphant and the Irkeasel

MONKEY PIRATE POINTS: 4.5 (out of 5)

NAME: Poppycock

RANK: (Not very) Able-Bodied Crewmember

DISTINGUISHING FEATURES: 1 wooden leg, 1 eye patch and 1 hook, false wooden teeth and a false tin ear

LIKES: Bananas and doing impressions of a monkey on a stick

FAVOURITE GAMES:
Fruit Fly Whack!! and Peel That Banana,
Mr McGinnty!!

FEARS: Meeting himself or his complete opposite in
some time-travel incident, plus poetry

AMBITION: To have a spare set of wooden teeth for
special occasions

MONKEY PIRATE POINTS: 4.5 (out of 5)

NAME: Piffle

RANK: A Banana Scallywag

LIKES: Bananas, grog, scratching
himself and good luck charms

PIFFLE

DISTINGUISHING FEATURES:

Believes that most things are bad luck

SAYINGS: "Aaaaargh! that be bad luck!" and "I tell ye, that be bad luck"

MOST UNCOMFORTABLE MOMENT:

Spending some time in a barrel full of monkeys

FEAR: Most things

MONKEY PIRATE POINTS: 4 (out of 5)

NAME: Balderdash

RANK: A Thumping Good Monkey Pirate and the Banana Bosun

DISTINGUISHING (AND DISGUSTING) FEATURES:
A short fat Monkey Pirate with only a few teeth, all of various colours (black, brown and white)

SKILLS: Whacking things with his whacking stick

DISLIKES: Fruit flies

SAYINGS: " Dem bibblyschuck things. Cabbage bum creatures. I 'ates dem!"

MONKEY PIRATE POINTS: 4.5 (out of 5)

(More to come at some time in the future!)

A FAIRLY USEFUL GUIDE TO THE AUTHOR AND THE ILLUSTRATOR

Your very own guide to keep, offering a quick reference to the people who wrote and illustrated this here book. This bit should be kept handy in the event of seeing one of them in your street.

NAME: Mark Skelton

RANK: A Scribbler of Words

BORN: In a small house in Sussex with very little hair

NOW: Lives in a small house in Sussex with very little hair

QUESTION THAT COMES TO MIND:
Why so many years but no change in the hair allocation?

CREW: 1 x wife (Amanda) and 1 x daughter (Emily)

RANK OF CREW: Both smashers!!

EDUCATION: Went to school with hair, went on to college with hair and then went to do a degree in Birmingham with lots of hair

143

WORK BACKGROUND:

First job as a civil servant working in a Job Centre with slightly less hair and then worked in magazine publishing with even less hair

CONCLUSION: Work isn't good for your hair!!!

LIKES: All pleasant children and biscuits

DISLIKES: Rice-pudding

AMBITION: To buy a wig

NAME: Ben Redlich

RANK: Ink Lackey

BORN: At a very young age

NOW: Retired to a sub-tropical paradise (but only when eyes are closed)

CREW: *1* x very patient wife-to-be

RANK OF CREW: Undisputed Overlord

EDUCATION: Studied Animation for 3 years (didn't get certificates, but did leave with something much better [see 'Crew'])

WORK BACKGROUND: Cleaner of churches, filler of shelves, sewer of sock monkeys, and philatelist. Oh, and once worked two hours in a secondhand bookshop

LIKES: Fritters with spaghetti and mash

DISLIKES: Raw tomato

AMBITION: To breed exotic chickens and live in a Grant Wood painting

A BIT TO SAY

This bit is to help say:

'We will always remember you' to Dom.

'Thanks for being there when it really mattered'
to my Dad, Suzanne, family and friends.

'You lot are great' to all the children I know and
'You lot are probably great as well' to all the children
I don't know and 'Watch out!' to everyone reading this
but not paying attention to where they are going.

Most of all, this bit is to help say,
'I love you lots' to Amanda and of course Emily.

A MESSAGE TO EMILY FROM HER DAD

I wished that I could write a book and have it published.

You are now holding a wish come true . . .

Make sure some of yours come true!!